STONE SOUP

BY ANN McGOVERN

PICTURES BY WINSLOW PINNEY PELS

SCHOLASTIC INC.
New York Toronto London Auckland Sydney

ISBN 0-590-40298-6

12 11 10 9 8 7 6 5 4   6 7 8 9/8 0 1/9

Printed in the U.S.A.   24

For Christopher Lane

—A.M.

For Trot,
who would eat anything
and did.

—W.P.P.

YOUNG MAN was walking.
He walked and he walked.
He walked all night.
And he walked all day.

He was tired. And he was hungry.

At last he came to a big house.
"What a fine house," he said.
"There will be plenty of food
for me here."

He knocked on the door.

A little old lady opened it.
"Good lady," said the young man,
"I am very hungry.
   Can you give me something to eat?"

"I have nothing to give you,"
   said the little old lady.
"I have nothing in the house.
   I have nothing in the garden."
   And she began to close the door.

"Stop," said the young man.
"If you will not give me
   something to eat,
   will you give me a stone?"

"A stone?" said the little old lady.
"What will you do with a stone?
 You cannot eat a stone!"

"Ah," said the young man.
"I can make soup from a stone."

Now the little old lady had never heard of that.
Make soup from a stone?
Fancy that.

"There are stones in the road,"
 said the little old lady.

The young man picked up a round,
 gray stone.
"This stone will make wonderful soup,"
 he said.
"Now get me a pot."

The little old lady got a pot.
"Fill the pot with water
and put it on the fire,"
the young man said.

The little old lady did as she was told.
And soon the water was bubbling
in the pot.

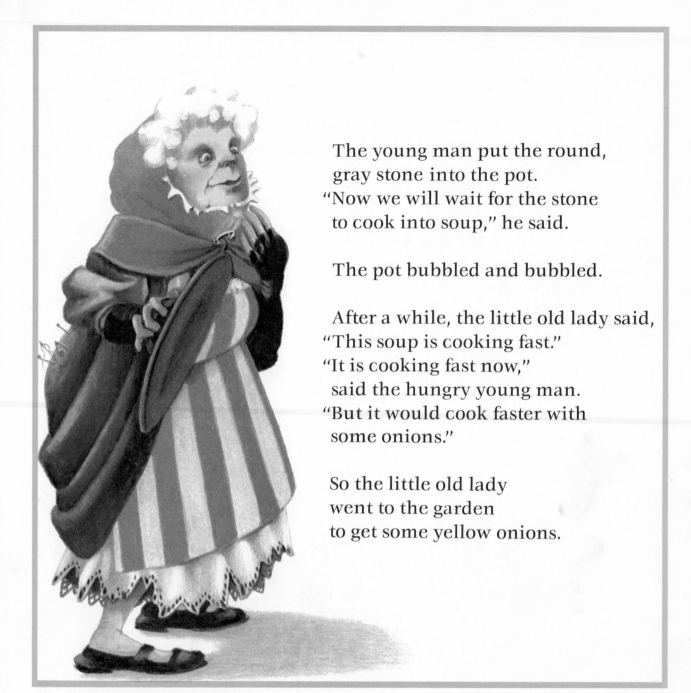

The young man put the round,
gray stone into the pot.
"Now we will wait for the stone
to cook into soup," he said.

The pot bubbled and bubbled.

After a while, the little old lady said,
"This soup is cooking fast."
"It is cooking fast now,"
said the hungry young man.
"But it would cook faster with
some onions."

So the little old lady
went to the garden
to get some yellow onions.

Into the pot went
the yellow onions,
with the round, gray stone.

"Soup from a stone," said the little
old lady.
"Fancy that."

The pot bubbled and bubbled.

After a while, the little old lady said,
"This soup smells good."

"It smells good now,"
said the hungry young man.
"But it would smell better with
some carrots."

So the little old lady went out to the garden
and pulled up all the carrots she could carry.

Into the pot went
the long, thin carrots,
with the yellow onions,
and the round, gray stone.

"Soup from a stone," said the little old lady.
"Fancy that."
The pot bubbled and bubbled.

After a while, the little old lady said,
"This soup tastes good."

"It tastes good now,"
said the hungry young man.
"But it would taste better
with beef bones."

So the little old lady went to get
some juicy beef bones.

Into the pot went
the juicy beef bones,
and the long, thin carrots,
and the yellow onions,
and the round, gray stone.

"Soup from a stone," said the little old lady.
"Fancy that."

The pot bubbled and bubbled.

After a while, the little old lady said,
"This soup is fit for a prince."

"It is fit for a prince now,"
said the hungry young man.
"But it would be fit for a king
with a bit of pepper
and a handful of salt."

So the little old lady
got the pepper and the salt.

Into the pot went
the bit of pepper
and the handful of salt,
with the juicy beef bones,
and the long, thin carrots,
and the yellow onions,
and the round, gray stone.

"Soup from a stone,"
said the little old lady.
"Fancy that."

The pot bubbled and bubbled.

After a while the little old lady said,
"This soup is too thin."

"It is too thin now," said the hungry young man.
"But it would be nice and thick
 with some butter and barley."

So the little old lady
went to get butter and barley.

Into the pot went
the butter and barley,
with the bit of pepper and the handful of salt,
and the juicy beef bones,
and the long, thin carrots,
and the yellow onions,
and the round, gray stone.

"Soup from a stone,"
said the little old lady.
"Fancy that."

The pot bubbled and bubbled.

After a while, the little old lady
tasted the soup again.
"That is good soup," she said.

"Yes," said the hungry young man.
"This soup is fit for a king.
Now we will eat it."

"Stop!" said the little old lady.
"This soup is indeed fit for a king.
Now I will set a table fit for a king."
So she took out her best tablecloth
and her best dishes.

Then the little old lady
and the hungry young man
ate all the soup—

the soup made with
the butter and barley,
and the bit of pepper,
and the handful of salt,
and the juicy beef bones,
and the long, thin carrots,
and the yellow onions,
and the round, gray stone.

"Soup from a stone,"
  said the little old lady.
"Fancy that."

"Now I must be on my way,"
  said the young man.
  He took the stone out of the pot,
  and put it into his pocket.

"Why are you taking the stone?"
  said the little old lady.

"Well," said the young man.
"The stone is not cooked enough.
  I will have to cook it some more
  tomorrow."

And the young man said good-bye.

He walked on down the road.
He walked and he walked.
"What a fine supper
I will have tomorrow,"
he said to himself.

"Soup from a stone.
Fancy that."